Do you like to eat delicious vegetables and fruits - as they will help keep you healthy! I hope so, Enjoy Delly's story.

Marley and Ryan!

Shirley Castro
May 6, 2020

DELLY

and the

BEACH TOWN HEALTHY ALPHABET CHALLENGE

by Shirley Castro
illustrated by Christopher Castro

A
B
C
D
E
F
G
H
I
J

Printed by Jostens Printing and Publishing
Visalia, CA
ISBN-13: 978-0-9790307-5-8
ISBN-10: 0-9790307-5-7

Dr. Healthy Bird says,
"To be healthy,
pelicans should eat
fish, but humans
should eat lots of
fruits and vegetables!"

Delly landed fast, as always, and slid up to the open doorway of Chef Chauncy's kitchen. And, as always, he was so-o-o hungry. He had already spotted the bucket of fish by the door. Chef Chauncy often kept a bucket there with a few fish for Delly to snack on. Delly liked Chef Chauncy and Chef Chauncy liked him. And, they both **loved** food.

Today he found the chef sitting at his desk. "What's up, Chef C?" asked Delly. "Well," said the chef. "Remember when Dr. Healthy Bird told Stelly that pelicans, like people, should eat food that is good for them? *

* In Stelly and the Sticky, Gooey Taffy

I've been hearing about people everywhere who have been helping **kids** learn about eating healthy foods. Now, we're going to do something right here in Beach Town."

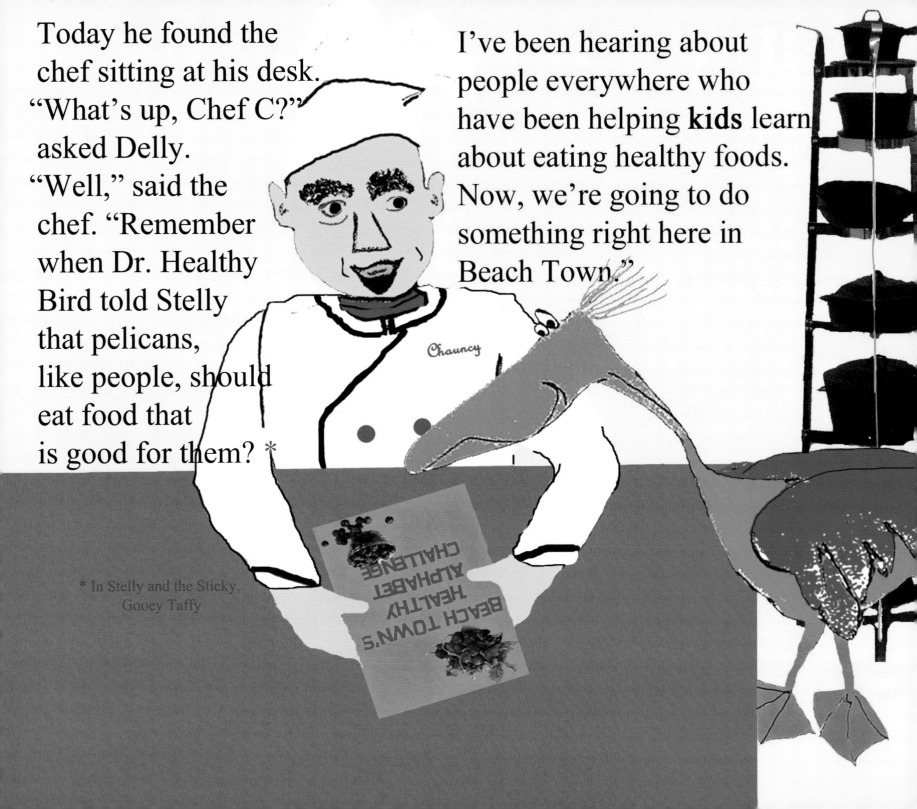

"Hey, Delly, I've got a great idea! We could use your footprint to make the stamp. The kids would love it. They know how much you like to eat!" "Sounds good to me." said Delly, "But could we do it quickly? I'm kind of in a hurry. I <u>have</u> to go out fishing. I'm so hungry I could eat a **whale!**"

Pelican feet, pelican feet,
Swimming feet,
Pelican feet!
Paddling great,
Walking straight
Warming feet,*
Pelican feet!

*Pelicans place
their webbed feet
over their eggs to
warm them.

The chef had some paint in the storeroom. He poured it into a paint tray. Delly stepped into it and onto a paper so the chef could get a print of his foot to make a stamp. Then Delly flew out over the ocean in search of some yummy fish to eat.

Fruits and vegetables are great for kids, but pelicans need fish!

Delly's slide-in landing at the school the next day brought a cheer from the students. Everyone had the Challenge Booklet in front of them and Chef Chauncy had just shown them the stamp they would get in their booklets when they tried the foods given to them. The first foods were:

Carlos had the blueberries in his hand, and was about to throw them at Ester, until he saw the chef. "Taste those," said the chef. "They're good."

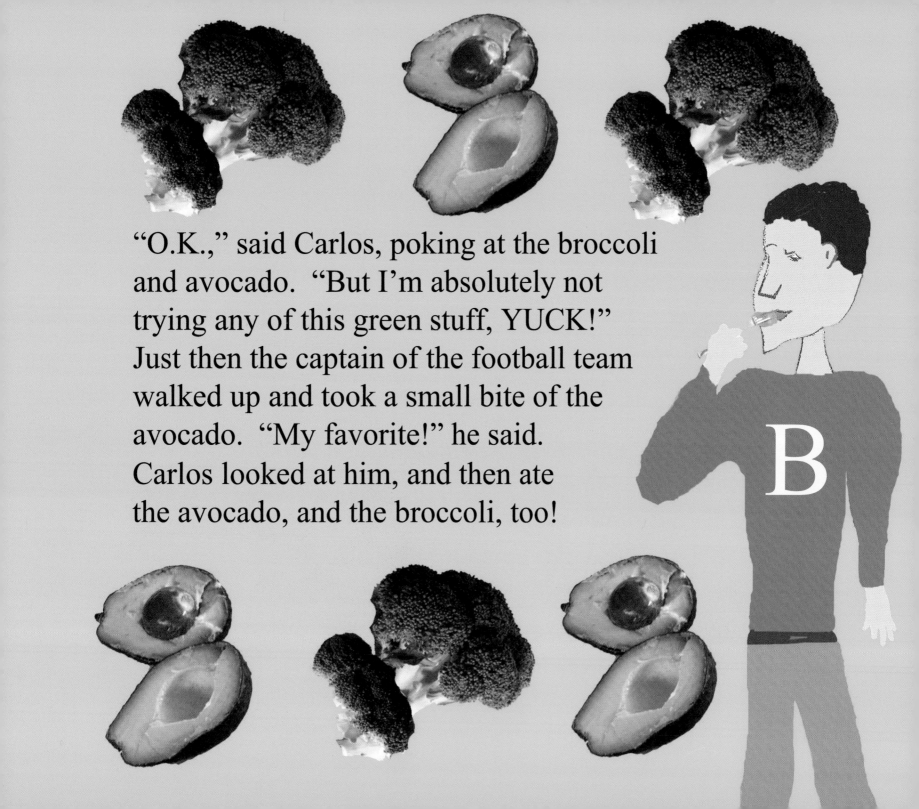

"O.K.," said Carlos, poking at the broccoli and avocado. "But I'm absolutely not trying any of this green stuff, YUCK!" Just then the captain of the football team walked up and took a small bite of the avocado. "My favorite!" he said. Carlos looked at him, and then ate the avocado, and the broccoli, too!

The next day, Candace didn't want to try the carrots. "Carlos may be O.K. with green stuff now, but I definitely don't like orange!" she said. "It's **not** my favorite color." Delly came by and encouraged her to try them. Reluctantly she agreed, and she found out she **did** like orange-colored vegetables.

"Hey!" yelled out Andy, holding up his cup. "Somebody gave me a dried beetle!"
"It's not a beetle," said Jacob. "It's a date, and it's delicious! If you don't want it, I'll eat it." Andy tasted it and sang out, "I'm eat-ing bee-tle guts," But he ate it all.

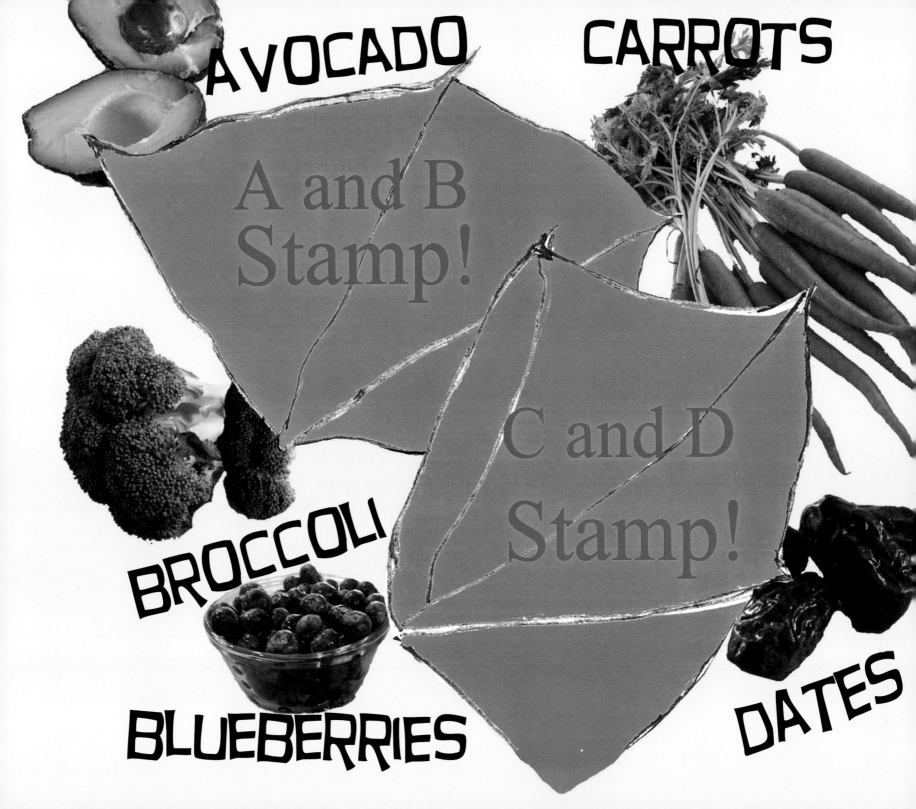

AVOCADO

CARROTS

A and B
Stamp!

C and D
Stamp!

BROCCOLI

BLUEBERRIES

DATES

Day three brought something different. When the students walked in, they saw slips of paper in one of their cups. There were pictures of people jumping rope, or running, or doing jumping jacks. "Pictures aren't fruits and vegetables,"said Alex with a smirk. "Someone made a mistake!"

"You're right," said Lin. "Pictures aren't fruits and vegetables, but exercise is part of being healthy."

"That's right," said Dr. Healthy Bird. When you go out to P.E. today and work hard doing jumping jacks, jumping rope, and running, you'll get today's stamp."

Then Elizabeth looked into the second cup. "E-e-e-u!" she squealed. "What's this?"
"It's a fig," said Dr. Bird. "and it has vitamins and minerals. And, it tastes sweet. Try it."
Elizabeth took a nibble. Her mom had told her she needed vitamins and minerals, so she ate it all.

Dr. Bird

EXERCISE

E and F Stamp!

FIGS

By day four, most of the kids were interested in the challenge, and couldn't wait to see what was being served next.

The cups were filled with grapes and Honeydew melon, which were eaten up quickly!

HONEYDEW MELON

G and H Stamp!

GRAPES

ICEBERG LETTUCE

This is Romaine Lettuce. It has more vitamins than Iceberg. (But it doesn't start with "I".)

I and J Stamp!

JICAMA

The teachers weren't sure if the kids would like the crispy kale with lemon yogurt dip. But when Aunt Melinda Bell walked by the students and picked several to come up front and help make the dip, everyone wanted to taste it.

Dr. Healthy Bird explained how dark green, leafy vegetables were really good for people!

lettuce   kale
spinach
collard greens   swiss chard

KALE

LEMON

K and L
Stamp!

Next, mango and nectarine smoothies
were made at each table by teachers with their blenders.
They were a hit! The first graders made up
a Mango Bango dance to show everyone.
The Beach Town Middle School Trumpeters played
while they danced. Delly even joined in,
which  made everyone laugh.

MANGO

NECTARINE

M and N

Stamp!

Wednesday of the second week was
Oranges, Onions and Peppers Day,
presented by the librarian, whose name was Pepper Brown.
There were sweet juicy oranges, and onions, and
red, yellow, orange, and green peppers, both sweet and hot!
Chef Chauncy cooked up some of the sweet peppers with onions
and put them on top of beans in tortillas for the students to try.

Yum!

ORANGES

O and P Stamp!

ONIONS

PEPPERS

Quince jelly on crackers and radishes were the next day's foods, using the radishes that the third grade students had planted earlier that year.

Many of the students had never heard of quince, but they were willing to try the jelly; and they loved it when Delly came flying in with the basket of radishes straight from the garden, and put them on the table in front of the chef.

QUINCE

Q and R
Stamp!

RADISHES

There were two foods for S -- beautiful, dark- green spinach and sweet strawberries.
For T there were tomatoes of several different colors: red, orange, yellow and greenish.

STRAWBERRIES

SPINACH

TOMATOES

S and T
Stamp!

Do any fruits or vegetables start with U and V?
There are some, but in the Beach Town Challenge,
U stands for
UTTERLY DELICIOUS CITRUS!
V stands for
VEGETABLES! VEGETABLES!
(green ones)

Wow! I didn't know lemons were so sour!

So on the U and V day, there were
different kinds of citrus-- like limes,
lemons, oranges, mandarins, and tangerines;
and different kinds of green vegetables --
like asparagus, brussel sprouts, celery,
green beans, and green onions.

The kids tasted those, and got their
pelican foot stamp for U and V.
Then came tasting for
W, X, Y, and Z, and the end
of the tasting challenge.

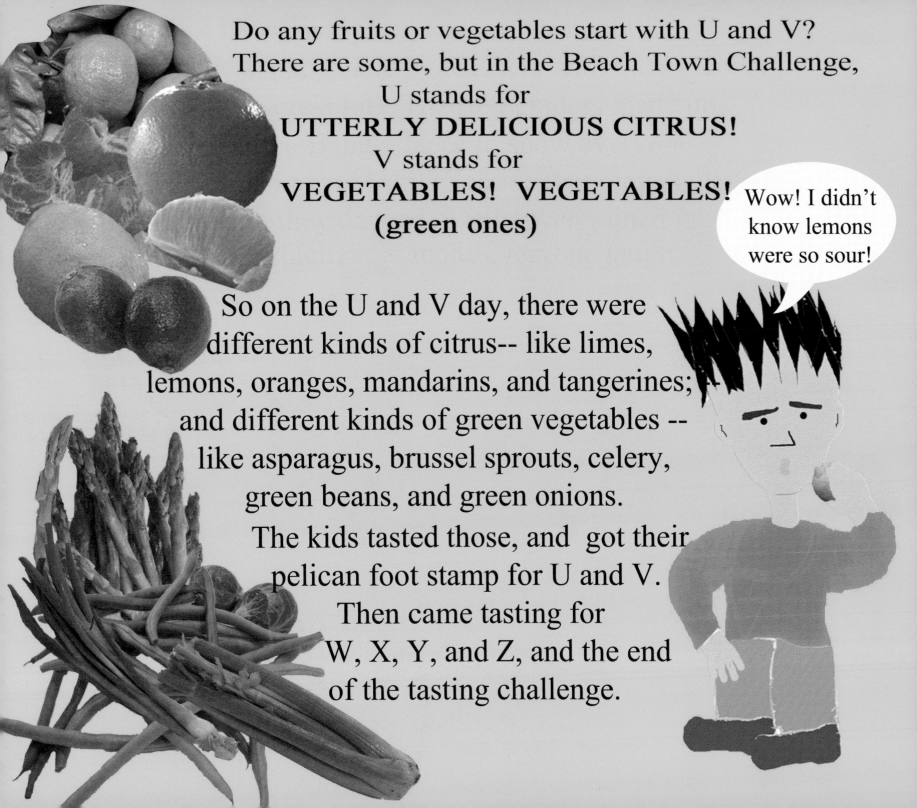

UTTERLY DELICIOUS CITRUS!

lemon
lime
mandarin
orange
tangerine

asparagus
brussel sprouts
celery
green beans
green onions

VEGETABLES! (GREEN ONLY)

U and V Stamp!

WATERMELON

EXTRA VEGETABLES

W and X Stamp!

Y and Z Stamp!

YAMS

ZUCCHINI

Chef Chauncy, Dr. Healthy Bird, and Delly were surprised when a big box arrived at the chef's office the next week, with a pelican made out of fruits and vegetables and a card from the students of Beach Town School that said, "Thanks for the Challenge! **We love fruits and vegetables!**"

"Wow!" said Delly, "The Challenge was a success! But I'm starving! I'm headed off to find some fish." And off he flew to join his friends, flying over the ocean, flying over the sea.

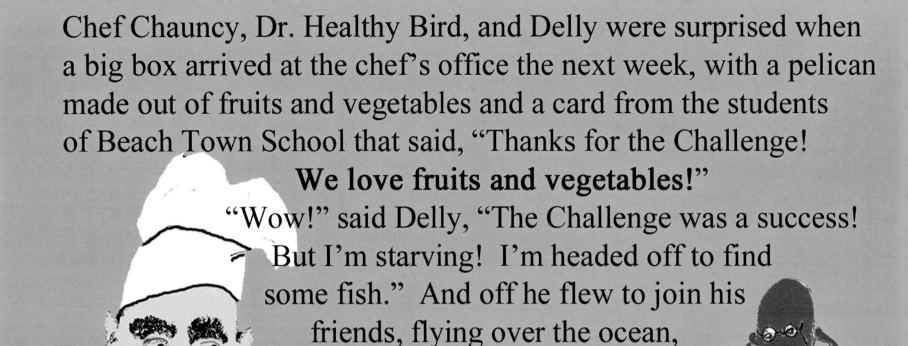

Delly and Chef Chauncy have shown you a few of the wonderful vegetables and fruits that you can eat that are delicious and good for you. Animals that live in and near the ocean have a different kind of "Healthy Alphabet". On the next two pages some things they might eat are listed. People eat some of these, too. Which ones do you like?

Ocean Plant or Animal	What Eats It
Algae	Sea Urchins
Barnacles	Mussels, Starfish
Crabs	Seagulls
Diatoms (a type of algae)	Krill
Eel	Elephant Seals
Fish	Sea animals, Birds
Grunion (a small fish)	Larger Fish, Birds
Herring (a small fish)	Salmon
Iophon sponge (a sea animal)	Some types of SeaStars
Jellyfish	Sea Turtles, Large Fish
Krill (small crustaceans)	Baleen Whales
Limpet (a type of snail)	Crabs, SeaStars, Birds
Mollusks(a very LARGE group of animals which includes Snails, Oysters, Squid, and Octopus)	Lots of different ocean animals

Ocean Plant or Animal	What Eats It
Nautilus(an animal with a coiled shell and tentacles)	Sea Turtles, Trigger Fish
Oysters	Sea Stars
Plankton	Krill, Baleen Whales
Quillfish	Salmon
Ray	Elephant Seals
Sea Stars or Star Fish	Seagulls
Tuna	Sharks
Urchins	Otters
Vampire Squid	Sea Lions, Whales
Whale	Delly said that he could eat a Whale, but that's not true.
Xiphosura (horseshoe crab)	Seagulls, Sea Turtles, Sharks
Yellowtail	Barracuda, Shark
Zooplankton	All kinds of ocean animals, including Whales

From the author:

When I was working on this book, I looked on the internet to get more ideas. For fruit and vegetable ideas I typed in "lists of fruits and vegetables" and got several different choices to use. I also looked up nutritional value of the fruits and vegetables I chose. When I got to the part of ocean animals and what they eat, I typed in "lists of ocean animals," and then typed in questions like "What eats Algae?" or "What does a Sea Star eat?" It was fun to learn more about ocean and seashore animals and plants.

Working on this book reminded me of how beautiful and delicious fruits and vegetables are. Since you are reading the last page of our book, I hope you think so, too. Taking the photos of all the fruits and veggies was fun, but eating them was even better!

Make your own Healthy Alphabet Challenge Book by putting together some blank pages and writing the letters of the alphabet on them. Leave room between the letters to put photographs, pictures you cut out of magazines (with your parents' permission) or drawings of the fruits and vegetables that start with each letter. You could even write down how you prepared them to eat and how well you liked them. Tell which members of your family liked each one.

We'd love to hear about your own healthy challenge. Let us know about your book by writing us at pelicancounting@aol.com, or commenting on our Facebook page--The Pelican Family Series. Have fun, and eat healthy foods!

This is book #5 in The Pelican Family Series.
You can find out about our other books at
www.pelicanfamily.com.
Also, please "like" us on Facebook -- The Pelican Family Series